PUFFIN BOOKS

The Headmaster's G
Juniors

Handles & Spouts Inc
is a secret club. Its mer
Amy, and their friends Mini, Ben and Ludo. All five
go to Jug Valley Juniors.

Mr Morton, the headmaster at Jug Valley
Juniors, has certainly not been his usual reliable
self lately. Hands think it odd when Ben's pottery
mug disappears from outside Mr Morton's office,
instead of being awarded the gold star that Ben
was promised. But then they hear that Mr
Morton shouted at one of the parents and threw
chocolate biscuits everywhere at Parents' Evening.
What can be the matter with him?

The mystery deepens when, the next day, Mr
Morton claims he wasn't at Parents' Evening. It
begins to look as though he may have to resign, so
Hands decide to find out what really happened.

This is the second of the enthralling books about
the adventures of Hands and its members at Jug
Valley County Junior School.

Anne Digby was born in Kingston-upon-Thames,
Surrey, but has lived in the West Country for many
years.

Other books by Anne Digby

BOYS v. GIRLS AT JUG VALLEY JUNIORS

The TREBIZON stories

FIRST TERM AT TREBIZON
SECOND TERM AT TREBIZON
SUMMER TERM AT TREBIZON
BOY TROUBLE AT TREBIZON
MORE TROUBLE AT TREBIZON
THE TENNIS TERM AT TREBIZON
SUMMER CAMP AT TREBIZON
INTO THE FOURTH AT TREBIZON
THE HOCKEY TERM AT TREBIZON
FOURTH YEAR TRIUMPHS AT TREBIZON
THE GHOSTLY TERM AT TREBIZON
FIFTH YEAR FRIENDSHIPS AT TREBIZON

The JILL ROBINSON stories

ME, JILL ROBINSON AND THE
   TELEVISION QUIZ
ME, JILL ROBINSON AND THE SEASIDE
   MYSTERY
ME, JILL ROBINSON AND THE
   CHRISTMAS PANTOMIME
ME, JILL ROBINSON AND THE SCHOOL
   CAMP ADVENTURE
ME, JILL ROBINSON AND THE PERDOU
   PAINTING
ME, JILL ROBINSON AND THE STEPPING
   STONES MYSTERY

The
Headmaster's Ghost
at Jug Valley Juniors

Anne Digby
Story devised with **Alan Davidson**

Illustrated by
Piers Sanford

PUFFIN BOOKS

PUFFIN BOOKS

Published by the Penguin Group
Penguin Books Ltd, 27 Wrights Lane, London W8 5TZ, England
Penguin Books USA Inc., 375 Hudson Street, New York, New York 10014, USA
Penguin Books Australia Ltd, Ringwood, Victoria, Australia
Penguin Books Canada Ltd, 10 Alcorn Avenue, Toronto, Ontario, Canada M4V 3B2
Penguin Books (NZ) Ltd, 182–190 Wairau Road, Auckland 10, New Zealand

Penguin Books Ltd, Registered Offices: Harmondsworth, Middlesex, England

First published 1992
10 9 8 7 6 5 4 3 2 1

Printed in England by Clays Ltd, St Ives plc
Filmset in Monophoto Baskerville

Contents

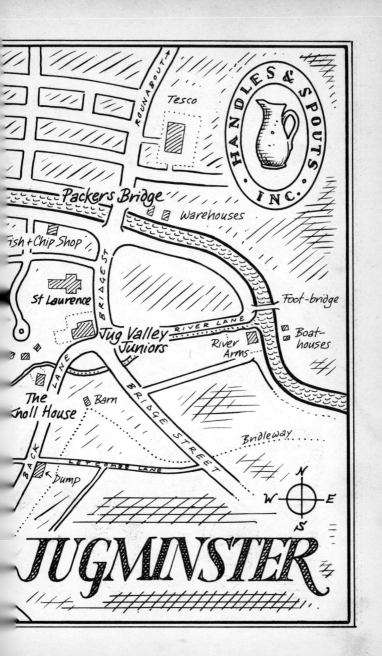

To Daniel

chapter 1

Parents' Evening

Mr Morton, the headmaster, was not
quite himself lately. Tim and Amy
Dalladay had both noticed it. Tim and
Amy were twins and were in 6A, the top
class at Jug Valley County Junior School.

Everybody respected Mort. He had a
deep, friendly voice and was always very
reliable. He was quite plump, with a bushy
brown beard. He liked to wear thick
brown clothes – comfortable ones. He
looked rather like a nice bear.

But lately he'd been more like a bear
with a sore head.

On Wednesday morning in assembly, he
actually shouted at them.

It was after he'd talked about Parents'
Evening. There were to be no afternoon
lessons. They were all to help their
teachers get the classrooms ready. There

would be no team practice after school. This led to a babble of noise in the hall. Whisper, whisper! Chatter, chatter! Parents' Evening!

'*Silence!*' he roared suddenly. He'd gone quite pale. 'That will *do*!'

The hall instantly became hushed. It was such a surprise, Mr Morton shouting like that. He never shouted at them as a rule.

'That's better.' His cheeks regained their proper colour. What a relief.

'One last announcement,' he said. He gazed along the rows of pupils, all seated cross-legged on the floor. 'How many of you have earned a gold star this week? Hands up, please.'

Mr Morton usually gave out gold stars on a Friday. Only exceptional work earned a headmaster's gold star. Very few hands went up. But one of them was Ben Brown's, because of his pottery mug.

Ben was chuffed. So were four of his classmates in 6A. The twins themselves; Amy's best friend Mary Minter (nicknamed Mini); and Ludovic (Ludo) Johnson.

Tim, Amy, Mini, Ludo and Ben were quite thick. Not thick meaning stupid. (In

fact Ludo and Mini were both very brainy.
Ludo was the school chess champion.)
Thick meaning close. They'd started a
secret club, called Handles & Spouts
Incorporated; Handles were the boys and
Spouts the girls. This name tended to get
shortened to H. AND S., or simply
Hands.

Handles & Spouts HQ was an old
yellow caravan at the bottom of the
Dalladays' orchard, by the stream. Ben
had already promised *the mug* to Club HQ.
They only had four, so they needed
another one.

For the fine work that had earned Ben
his first-ever headmaster's gold star was a
smart brown glazed pottery mug. The
other four all agreed that it was a work of
genius.

Even Elizabeth Vine's mother, who was
a real potter, was very impressed. Mrs
Vine owned the Jugminster Pottery in
Cheap Street. A group from 6A had been
to her workshop. She'd shown them how
to work the clay and throw it, using the
potter's wheel. They'd all tried to make
something.

Only Ben's mug had turned out right.
Ben was big for his age, with large, strong

hands. Later, Mrs Vine had fired it in her
kiln. Then she'd shown Ben how to paint
it and glaze it. He'd brought the finished
article to school yesterday afternoon,
Tuesday.

'Ben, it looks like a proper mug!' Amy
had exclaimed in disbelief.

'It *is* a proper mug!' he'd laughed.

'Big-head,' muttered Marcus King. He'd
tried to make a bowl, himself. It had
turned out all wobbly and wavy. He stared
at Ben's mug. 'That was just fluky.'

'And you're just spooky,' said Ludo.

'And puky!' added Tim.

Marcus King was in a bad mood on Tuesday. He'd been told that he hadn't won the Environmental Studies prize, as he'd confidently expected to. It had gone to a Year Five girl. He was hoping his mother wouldn't come to school and make a scene about it. She was always interfering, just because she was a Parent Governor.

Soon after this their class teacher, Mr Gage, examined the handsome piece of brown pottery carefully. He decided that it should have a headmaster's gold star. He filled in a special slip, signed it and handed it to Ben.

'Leave this in Mrs Hart's office, with your piece of pottery, before you go home. She'll make sure it gets a gold star from Mr Morton tomorrow. In time for Parents' Evening. Well done, Ben!'

So now Ben Brown had his hand up in assembly, on Wednesday morning.

'Good,' said Mr Morton, looking at the raised hands. 'I'm giving out gold stars early this week, so that your parents can see them on show this evening. Please bring gold star work to Mrs Hart's office after assembly. And please make sure that your teachers have signed your slips. I'll go through each item today. They'll be ready for collection this afternoon.'

Ben lowered his hand. He glanced at Tim and gave a pleased little shrug.

He'd already done all that. He'd taken the stuff to Mrs Hart's office at home-time, yesterday. Mrs Hart, the school secretary, had left. Ben hadn't liked to knock on the door of the inner office, the headmaster's. So he'd left the mug and slip on the trolley in the outer office, right next to Mrs Hart's desk.

His work would be the first in the queue for a gold star. He'd collect it this afternoon, when they'd finished getting the classroom ready.

That should keep Mum and Dad happy this evening!

It was fun that afternoon, getting Room 6A ready. It was a large classroom with big windows. They overlooked the playground. A dense hedge separated the playground from the school's green sports field. The hedge was lush with red berries and hips, dark purple sloes and blue-black elderberry clusters. Amy and Mini had gone to cut some, to make a display.

While they were outside, in the pale

watery sunshine, they talked about the headmaster.

He'd just backed his white car out of its special parking bay by the school hall, then driven off through the gates. They'd waved to him but he hadn't waved back.

'I wonder where he's going?' said Amy.

'To get his suit from the cleaners, maybe,' replied Mini. Mr Morton only wore a suit on special occasions, like Parents' Evenings. It was always the same one. Quite jazzy, with brown and white checks.

'He's funny lately, isn't he,' mused Amy.

'Kate Roberts says he's got troubles at home!' shrugged Mini. 'She says her mum heard him quarrelling with his family in the chemist.'

'Oh, trust Kate,' said Amy. 'That's just silly.'

'Hey,' said Tim, when they went back into the classroom, 'you can't put those berries there. They'll hide my rainfall map.'

'Sorry, Tim. OK, we'll move them along here.'

The classroom looked great. All their maths and English books were open on their tables, for the parents to inspect. Specially good work was displayed on the work-bench. This included Amy's English project about her favourite author and Marcus King's Environmental Studies' project about the River Jug. There was a space left for Ben's mug. (He'd gone to collect it.) And there was a lot more stuff blu-tacked along the wall, above the work-bench.

Tim gazed at his rainfall map there, relieved to see it up. It didn't look much beside some of Ludo and Mini's work. But it was better than nothing!

Where had Ben got to? Tim wondered. It was nearly home-time.

By the time Ben came back, nearly everyone had gone home. Only his friends remained.

'About time, Ben!' said Mr Gage. 'But where's your pottery?'

'It's disappeared, sir! Someone must have taken it!'

Mrs Hart had seen no sign of it when she'd arrived at school this morning. It certainly wasn't on the trolley where Ben had left it. She'd now searched her entire office and looked in Mr Morton's as well. Perhaps the headmaster had noticed it, late on Tuesday afternoon? But she couldn't ask him because he'd left.

'Taken it? Don't be silly, Ben. I'll speak to the headmaster at Parents' Evening,' frowned Mr Gage. 'Oh, this is too bad. Mr Morton was working late yesterday; I expect he found it and put the gold star on then. But where is it now?'

'He's not coming back for Parents' Evening, sir,' Ben said, looking glum. He'd already checked. 'Mrs Edwards is standing in for him.' Mrs Edwards was the deputy head.

'Of course. You're right. He's got to go somewhere. Oh, this is too bad!' Mr Gage repeated. 'Well, there's nothing more can be done today.'

He shooed the five of them out of the classroom; the cleaners were waiting to come in.

As they all walked home along Back Lane, in a bunch, Ben took a flying kick at a stone. 'I still think somebody might have nicked it!' he said.

'Surely not, Ben,' protested Amy.

'I think we should meet and discuss,' rapped out Tim. His face darkened. '*Hands*. Six o'clock. OK?'

'What's there to discuss?' frowned Mini.

17

'It's obvious Mort's forgotten to give it to Mrs Hart. I know it's annoying, Ben, but that's all it is.'

'Mort's not usually forgetful!' said Ludo.

'And don't come if you don't want to!' retorted Tim.

'Oh, I'll come all right,' said Mini. 'I was only saying it doesn't seem much of a mystery!'

But there was a much bigger one to come.

chapter 2

A Fleeting Appearance

So they met at the caravan at six o'clock. They took their secret jug badges out of the drawer and pinned them on. It was part of the fun.

All their parents had disappeared off to school. Mr and Mrs Dalladay had taken Harry with them, in his push-chair. Harry was the twins' baby brother, aged two. He was wearing his new white track suit and looked clean and scrubbed.

'Do you *have* to take him?' Tim had grumbled, at the front gate.

'Of course we do,' said Mrs Dalladay. 'He's looking forward to it. He's had an extra nap.'

Harry was impatient. He was bouncing

up and down in his push-chair. He could
see people walking along Back Lane
towards the school. He was in a frenzy of
excitement.

'Harry doeing to school. Harry doeing
to school!'

'Are you two offering to look after him,
then?' asked Mr Dalladay solemnly.

Tim and Amy exchanged horrified
looks. Of course they weren't!

'Harry doeing to school!' the little boy
shrieked. His face crumpled. Instantly Tim
hugged him. Amy kissed him on top of his
brown curly head.

'Off you go, Harry. Be good!' she
laughed.

'Don't let us down!' said Tim. 'Like
your outfit, Harry. Really smart.'

Phew.

Now the five class-mates were in the
caravan. It was a pale yellow caravan, its
paint peeling from years of facing the open
sea at Mable Darcy. Dad had towed it
back home to the Knoll House and given
it to the twins. He'd deposited it as far
from the house as he possibly could. It sat
here on the bank of the stream, secretive,
half hidden in long grass and apple trees
and overhanging willow. It was Tim and

Amy's own den and they loved it down here. A notice on the door said:

HANDLES & SPOUTS
INCORPORATED
HQ
PRIVATE

It was a good meeting place; very convenient. Mini lived at 27 Back Lane, just across the road from the Dalladays. Ben and Ludo lived on the newish estate directly behind the grounds of the Knoll

House. The same stream bounded their own back gardens. They'd made a foot-bridge and could get to the HQ from their houses in less than a minute.

'Handles & Spouts go into emergency session, then,' smiled Amy, as she pinned on her badge.

'It's not funny,' grumbled Ben. 'Now Mum and Dad haven't got anything to look at except my messy English books.'

'And we're still a mug short!' said Ludo. He'd found a large bottle of coke in the fridge at home and brought it across. 'You can swig yours from the bottle, Mini, as you don't think this mystery's important.' He kept a straight face as he said it. It was difficult to know *what* Ludo was thinking.

'Gagey'll tell your mum and dad all about your ace mug, Ben,' said Tim, to cheer him up. He frowned. 'But that's not the point.'

Ludo had the club notebook and pencil.

'Let's enumerate,' he said. He started to write. 'Missing: one mug.' He looked up. 'Discuss!'

They had plenty of theories. Some of them sensible, some not. They talked for ages. As time went on, the theories got wilder. It was Tim, at last, who called a halt.

'That's really daft, Amy! And if one of the cleaners *had* watered Mrs Hart's pot plant with Ben's mug, it'd still be there!'

'I think it boils down to theories number 1, 2 or 3,' said Ludo.

'Agreed. Read them out then,' said Tim.

Ludo read from the notebook as follows:

1: Ben had enemy. *Prime suspect:* Marcus King. *Action:* Ask around. Search M.K.'s locker? If guilty, bop on the nose.

2: Mort inspected mug late yesterday. Awarded gold star. Forgot to give it back to Mrs Hart today. *Action:* Deputation to head – Ben and Amy. Tact needed.

3: Person unknown nicked mug. Took a fancy to it. *Action:* If blank drawn with (1) and (2), then Hands investigate. Was anyone seen coming out of Mrs Hart's office late Tuesday p.m. or early Wednesday a.m.?

'I still think it's number 2,' said Mini.

'Maybe,' agreed Ludo.

Ben looked at his watch. Some of them started to think about Parents' Evening. It would be over by now. Better go home, hear the worst.

The meeting broke up.

Tim and Amy were the last to leave the caravan.

'Wonder how things went at school?' said Tim, putting it into words. He knew his father would have looked at his maths books. Mr Dalladay designed computer systems for a living. He was hot on maths. 'Hope Dad liked my rainfall map.'

'Let's go and find out,' said Amy, running through the dewy grass. 'Look, they're back!'

At least, Harry was. They could see his small figure standing on the back step. He couldn't open the kitchen door because his hands were full. He was waiting to be let in.

'Harry!' groaned Tim as they led him indoors, into the light. 'Did you have to?'

'That was very naughty, Harry,' scolded Amy.

Two pudgy handfuls of melting chocolate biscuits were pressed to his chest. His clean white tracksuit was now a total mess.

The twins had last seen the chocolate biscuits piled high on big plates, in the school hall – on a long table, with lots of coffee-cups – ready for Parents' Evening.

24

Harry contorted his face and made a glugging noise.

'And *what* have you got in your mouth?' asked Amy, in alarm. 'You're all gummed up!'

She knelt down, opened Harry's mouth, and gently eased something out. It was a large sweet, black-and-white striped.

'Yum!' said Tim. 'It's a Minty Monster! They sell them in Jugmouth. Hey, you're not supposed to have those, Harry.' He took it from Amy and licked it. 'Haven't had one of these for ages!'

'Don't be disgusting, Tim. Who ever gave it to you, Harry?' asked Amy. 'It's lucky you didn't choke.'

Their little brother laughed. He'd had it in his mouth since a quarter-past seven and it was now half-past. It was such a relief to get rid of it!

'Father Christmas,' he pronounced.

'Don't tell fibs, Harry,' said Tim. The little boy was now lining the smudged-looking chocolate biscuits in a row, on the kitchen table.

'Did,' said Harry stubbornly. He suddenly threw a chocolate biscuit up in the air and watched it land on the floor. 'An' shocklet biscuits!' he laughed.

'Harry – !' began Amy.

The back door opened and Mum and Dad came in with the empty push-chair.

They'd been deep in conversation with Mini's mother, at the front gate, and had let Harry run ahead. They looked a bit unsmiling.

'Did you see Amy's project?' asked Tim anxiously.

'Did you see Tim's good map?'

But Mr and Mrs Dalladay's minds seemed to be on something else.

'Smashing map, Tim,' said Dad. He frowned. 'And your project, Amy. Liked it.'

'What did Mr Gage say about us?' asked Amy, longing to know.

'Oh, nothing much,' said Mum, abstractedly. It was a relief; yet not very satisfying. 'I've forgotten for the minute. Don't look so worried!'

'He seemed quite pleased with you both,' Dad pointed out.

Phew! thought Tim.

'What's wrong then, Mum?' asked Amy.

'Well, it was Mr Morton – ' replied Mrs Dalladay.

'Did he come after all?' asked Tim in surprise.

'Right at the end. We were drinking our coffee. The hall was nearly empty. It was just a fleeting appearance!' Mum looked worried. 'It was *most* peculiar . . .'

Mr Dalladay shot his wife a warning look.

'He wasn't himself!' Dad cut in, to silence her. 'Feeling ill, I expect. Now, Harry, you're not to eat those biscuits. You *know* they've been on the floor.'

'Shocklet biscuits!' pleaded Harry. 'Father Christmas!'

'Don't be silly, baby,' said Mum. 'That wasn't Father Christmas – '

Suddenly Tim thought of the headmaster's bushy beard.

'Oh! Does little bruv mean Mr Morton gave him the biscuits?'

'Cut it out, Tim,' said his father. 'Leave the subject alone.'

He scooped up the biscuits and put them in the waste bin.

Tim and Amy looked at one another, mystified. What on earth had happened at Parents' Evening?

chapter 3
Odder and Odder

*M*ini's mother always told her things.
She was divorced and there were just the
two of them. By the time Mini left their
little thatched cottage on Thursday
morning, she knew everything.

It was sensational.

She told Amy on the way to school.
Then the five of them went into a huddle
in the playground, before the bell. Mini
swore them to secrecy.

According to Mrs Minter, the check-
suited headmaster had appeared in the
hall 'like a puff of smoke'. There'd been
no sign of his white car outside. One
minute he was smiling strangely and
greeting people. The next, he was shouting

and waving his arms around and throwing chocolate biscuits up in the air!

'What happened then?' asked Ben, in a hushed voice.

'Well, general confusion. People ducking and dodging biscuits,' said Mini. 'One hit Mum on the nose and Marcus King's mum spilt her coffee. By the time they'd recovered, he'd gone. Vanished!'

Tim nudged Amy and they both nodded. Now everything was clear. Harry's biscuits. Father Christmas. Dad refusing to speak about it.

'Didn't anyone hear his car drive away?' asked Tim, always practical.

'There wasn't any car,' insisted Mini.

'Must have been a poltergeist,' said Ludo solemnly.

'What's that, Ludo?' asked Amy, slightly fearful.

'It's a kind of ghost that throws things,' replied Ludo.

'Don't be stupid, Lu!' said Ben. 'Stop trying to scare Amy!'

'You must be joking!' exclaimed Mini, forgetting to keep her voice down. 'You don't think we believe in ghosts, do you?'

'What ghosts?' asked Kate Roberts, who was passing.

'M.Y.O.B.!' retorted Ben.

'Oh, all right then. I was only asking!' giggled Kate, joining the crush into school. First bell had gone.

'Well, at least the news hasn't got around,' said Tim, as they followed at a safe distance.

'Perhaps it'll just blow over,' said Amy hopefully.

They thought the world of Mr Morton. He was utterly, totally sensible, even if not quite himself lately. You just couldn't imagine him doing anything silly! The whole thing was fantastic. They felt worried about him; protective.

'If Kate Roberts doesn't know,' said Ludo, 'then nobody knows.'

Not even the headmaster himself, it seemed.

Not according to what he said at assembly.

Handles & Spouts were struck by how relaxed Mr Morton looked. He was smiling at assembly, making jokes. One reason for this was that he'd had his best night's sleep for weeks. There were other reasons, too.

He was back to his usual self. No doubt about it.

But there was a shock in store.

'I hear yesterday evening was a great success,' he beamed, at the end of assembly. 'Several parents have told me at the gates this morning how impressed they were with your classrooms! Well done. Congratulations on all your hard work.'

Then came the astonishing statement:

'I'm very sorry indeed that I missed it all. This is the first Parents' Evening I've ever missed! I would like to have been able to put in an appearance.'

With that, he dismissed them.

The bottom juniors filed out first. Young Paula Harris and her friends whispered and gabbled together excitedly. The Harrises, like the Dalladays and Mrs Minter, had been amongst the last parents to leave yesterday evening. And just like them, they'd witnessed the amazing manifestation.

Eavesdropping last night (hoping to find out what her teacher had said about her), seven-year-old Paula had overheard the whole story. She'd already told all her friends.

The five top juniors were more discreet. Tim, Amy, Ben, Ludo and Mini marched silently out of the hall, expressionless. They wanted to hide their astonishment.

So did another top junior: Marcus King. He was rather pale, all the same.

Marcus wished with all his heart that his mother hadn't insulted the headmaster on his behalf. It was horrible. It was embarrassing. Now poor old Mort seemed to have wiped the whole episode from his mind. Who could blame him? But where was it all going to end?

Handles & Spouts reasoned differently. If Mort said he wasn't at school last night, then he wasn't.

Well, probably not.

The whole thing was getting odder and odder.

chapter 4

An Ace Case

'**C**ome on, Ben,' said Amy, at morning
break. She had him by the arm and was
pulling him along the corridor. 'Let's ask
Mr Morton about your mug. We said we
would!'

Tall, broad-shouldered Ben was
dragging his feet.

Of course, he'd given Marcus King the
third degree. Marcus had been in a very
funny mood this morning; very subdued.
But he'd denied all knowledge of the mug.
For the time being, Ben had lost interest
in it.

'Don't let's bother Mort, Amy. Not just
now. I expect it'll turn up.'

This new mystery was much more
important. Much more serious than an
old mug! He wanted time to think about
it.

'Come *on*, Ben!' exclaimed Amy, outside the school office. 'We're here now!'

And at that moment, the door opened and Mrs Hart appeared in the corridor. She was just going off somewhere, with a stack of work books.

'Hello, Ben!' she said brightly. 'Mr Morton's free at the moment. Would you like to go through?'

So that was it.

They walked through her room, past the famous trolley, towards the door of the inner office. Ben tapped politely.

'Enter!' said the headmaster.

He was sitting behind his desk, poring over some papers. He motioned them to wait. Amy stared at an old print of Jugminster Abbey on the wall. How lovely the abbey looked, covered in snow. Ben gazed at the faded photo next to it. It was of the headmaster in his youth, slim and light-haired in those days, without a beard. He was wearing a college track suit and holding up an athletics cup. Only the distinctive high cheek-bones and bushy eyebrows (though lighter coloured then) made him recognizable. Mort had certainly put on weight since he was at college! But his love of athletics was one of the things, in Ben's opinion, that made him a great headmaster.

Mort laid his papers to one side and looked up.

'Ah, Ben. Your pottery. This is most annoying, isn't it? Mrs Hart's spoken to me. As has your class teacher. Very, very annoying. An excellent piece of work, I gather. I'm afraid there's no sign of it, Ben.' His deep voice was full of sympathy. 'As you know, I looked at all the gold star work yesterday. There was no pottery amongst it. We shall have to do something about this.'

Ben just shuffled his feet, tongue-tied.

'Excuse me, sir,' Amy said determinedly, 'but it wouldn't have been with the other work. Ben left it by Mrs Hart's desk on Tuesday afternoon. Didn't you, Ben?'

'On the trolley, sir.'

Mort just shook his head and smiled.

'Mrs Hart has already explained that,' he said gently. 'I don't recollect seeing it, I'm afraid. However – ' He frowned and looked for paper and pencil. 'I'm very angry about this. The culprit must be found.'

He started to write a memo.

'I'll give out a notice in assembly tomorrow,' he promised. 'Now, Ben. Describe. What colour is it?' His pencil was poised.

'Well, sir, it's – '

Brrr – Brrr. The phone rang on Mr Morton's desk and he picked it up.

'Hello. Headmaster speaking.'

There was a crackling sound on the line.

'Good morning, Sir David!' responded the Head. He was beaming. 'What can I do for you?'

Sir David Grateley was the Chairman of the Governors. He was phoning from home. He lived in an Elizabethan house in the abbey close.

There was sustained crackling. At this end of the line, Mr Morton was no longer beaming.

Ben and Amy glanced at his face. It was turning pale. They didn't know what to do. Stay or go? They were frozen with embarrassment.

But Mort was no longer aware of them.

'I'm afraid Mrs King has made a mistake!' he said.

More crackling. Then –

'I'm sorry, Sir David. I was nowhere near Jug Valley Juniors last night. I was in no state to be so. I was with Mr Pomfret, my dental surgeon. Afterwards I drove straight home and went to bed.'

More crackling.

'No. There was nobody else at home. Just myself.'

A pause. Then –

'Other complaints?' Mr Morton's face was now completely white. Ben and Amy were edging towards the door, on tiptoe. This was awful! 'If you say so, Sir David . . . Three o'clock, Sunday. At your home? Will this be a full Governors' meeting? . . . Yes. I see. I'll be there.'

Looking dazed, Mr Morton replaced the telephone and sat gazing into space.

Ben and Amy managed to reach the door.

'Wait!' he rapped out.

He stared at them.

'Have either of your parents mentioned that I might have put in an appearance at school yesterday evening?' he asked.

'Mine haven't, sir!' said Ben, stoutly.

Amy just went bright red.

'All right, Amy. There's no need to answer my question,' said Mr Morton.

He looked earthquake-shaken.

'Your pottery, Ben,' he said, gathering himself together.

He noted down the details. Amy and Ben saw that the pencil was trembling as he wrote.

'I'll give it out in assembly tomorrow morning,' he repeated.

After that, Ben and Amy fled.

'I've never seen him so upset!' gasped Amy, when they reached the corridor. 'It's almost as though he thinks he *might* have been here last night!'

'Course not, Amy!' scoffed Ben, who seemed relieved. 'He was angry, that's all. He was at the dentist! Trust Marcus's mum to stir up trouble. Well, she's going to look a fool on Sunday when they hold the Governors' meeting. I expect Mort will bring signed proof from his dentist!'

'But if it wasn't him, who was it?' whispered Amy.

'Dunno,' shrugged Ben. 'Some joker or other, I suppose.'

'What, his exact double? In the same suit he wears and everything?' replied Amy.

She gave a little shiver. The bottom juniors were all saying that the headmaster had a ghost.

'Come off it, Amy,' grinned Ben, reading her mind. He briefly patted her on the shoulder. 'It wasn't *Mort*, that's all that matters.' He turned. 'Got to go to football now. Can't wait to tell Tim and Ludo!'

'And I must find Mini,' nodded Amy.

As Ben dashed off, she frowned, wishing the spooky feeling would go away.

Tim and Ludo were in the boys' changing room. Ben talked to them quite loudly because he felt pleased. None of them realized that Marcus King was just behind the lockers, lacing up his football boots.

As Ben finished telling the story, Marcus

appeared. He'd heard every word. Now there was no point in his keeping silent any longer. The story was out.

'Mr Morton was *not* at the dentist last night!' he said. He looked embarrassed. 'He was shouting at my mum. My mum was rude to him and he went crazy!'

'Shut up, King! It was somebody *else*!' hissed Ben, through gritted teeth.

'He's just pretending it wasn't him!' insisted Marcus. 'Otherwise he might get the sack. But that's weird. That's just making things worse. It was him all right. He must be cracking up or something.' Marcus looked quite sick about it, really. 'I expect you'll find he's got your rotten mug as well, Brown.'

Ben took a step towards him, fists clenched, wanting to hit him. Not because of the mug. But because Marcus was now suggesting that Mort was a coward, on top of everything else!

'If he said he was at the dentist, he was at the dentist!' exclaimed Tim angrily.

'I only wish he had been,' shrugged Marcus. He left the changing room.

The other three boys straightened their blue JVJ football shirts. They walked out to the sports field in silence. The

Handles didn't believe it. Not one word of it. But they could tell that Marcus did. And he seemed so sure.

'As long as he was at the dentist, he's got an alibi,' muttered Tim at last.

'He said it was Mr Pomfret,' said Ben, remembering.

'Pomfret?' exclaimed Ludo. 'Pomfret and Drew?' He punched the air in excitement. 'That's where Charlotte works! She's their receptionist!'

'Honest?' said Ben. Charlotte Hughes was best friends with Anya Johnson, Ludo's eldest sister. She'd decided not to go on to Jugmouth College with Anya, last year, but to stay in Jugminster and get a job. 'Hey! Think you can get round her, Lu?'

'Got to try,' said Ludo. 'Haven't I?'

Tim glared across at Marcus King. Marcus was limbering up with the ball, flicking a deft little pass to David Marshall.

'If you ask me, this is a really ace – '

The blast of the whistle drowned the rest of Tim's sentence.

'Come on, you three! Stop chatting!' yelled Mr Gage, who was taking football today. 'How long d'you think we've got? Till Sunday?'

The three boys exchanged startled looks. They almost laughed. That was *exactly* how long they'd got. Till Sunday. Because on Sunday their headmaster was going to be hauled up in front of the Governors!

It was a most peculiar mystery. Had somebody been getting at him?

It was possible, just possible, that he might need help.

Which meant they had to find out if he *had* got an alibi.

'A really ace case for Hands!' repeated Tim, as they ran on to the pitch together.

'And urgent!' added Ben.

chapter 5
Ludo's Theory

*T*hey went to Club HQ straight from
school, all five of them. They didn't even
bother with tea. They went down to the
caravan, with the Dalladays' radio-phone
and the Yellow Pages directory. They
needed those.

'Still engaged!' said Ludo, impatiently.
He switched the phone off. Pomfret &
Drew was Jugminster's biggest dental
surgery. Very busy. 'And they shut at
half-past four! That's what it says in the
Yellow Pages.'

Ludo wanted to catch Charlotte while
she was still at work. Sitting at the little
reception desk, with the Appointments'
Book open in front of her.

'But they shut later on Wednesdays!'
Ben reminded them, looking pleased. It
said that in the Yellow Pages, too: *Evening*

Surgery on Wednesdays: 6–8 p.m. A good sign, that.

'Oh, Mort was there last night, all right,' said Mini, confidently. 'You'll see.'

'So we're all hoping,' said Ludo.

'What are you on about?' asked Tim.

'Well, think about it, you numbskulls,' replied Mini. 'Something's been making him a bit fragile lately. What?'

Amy and Mini had discussed it that morning. It was Mini who'd thought of it.

'His teeth have been hurting!' explained Amy. 'That's why he shouted in assembly yesterday, and he was in too much pain to go to Parents' Evening. He *had* to go to the dentist. And by this morning's assembly, he was fine again. His old self.'

'Whatever the trouble was, Mr Pomfret's fixed it!' said Mini. 'It all fits.'

'It does, doesn't it?' mused Tim.

'Why didn't we think of that?' wondered Ben.

'One up to Spouts!' admitted Ludo. 'What's known as inspiration. But we've still got to check the facts.'

'Perhaps he had gas!' whispered Mini. 'Perhaps he didn't know what he was doing afterwards!'

Ludo pressed the redial on the radio-phone.

At last – the ringing tone!

They all held their breaths and leant forward. Someone answered the phone.

'Good afternoon, dental surgery.'

'Charlotte, is that you?' Ludo licked his lips because they'd gone all dry. 'It's Ludo here – Ludo Johnson.'

'Only one Ludo in town!' laughed Charlotte. 'Want to make an appointment?'

'No, it's not that. Char, can you help about something? Did Mr Pomfret see Mr Morton last night?'

'As a matter of fact, yes. But – '

'What time did Mort leave?'

'Now, look here, Ludo – '

'Please, Char! It's *really* important.'

'Seven. Exactly.'

'How d'you know that?'

'Because I do. And what's this all about, Ludo? I'm not answering any more questions.'

'Look, Char. It's just that he might have lost something,' pleaded Ludo. 'Did he have gas?'

'No, he did not have gas!' said Charlotte, crossly. 'You mean he's asked you to ring up for him?' She sounded baffled. 'Well, he didn't leave anything here. OK?'

'Fine!' said Ludo. His hands were perspiring. 'Look, forget it, Char. That's all! See ya, then. Bye.'

'Bye! Give my love to Anya! Tell her I'm looking forward to Saturday!'

On Saturday night, Ludo's sister was appearing in a Shakespeare play at college.

As he rang off, Mini nudged him.

'You liar!' she said to him.

'So Mort *did* go to the dentist!' exclaimed Amy.

47

But the boys looked anxious.

'What time did he leave, Lu?'

'Seven o'clock,' replied Ludo. He was thoughtful. 'So where does that leave us?'

He gazed around at the others, who were all frowning in concentration.

'The – er – apparition at school. What time was it?'

Amy hated Ludo using that word; it made her flesh creep.

'Well, it was near the end,' she said. 'But we don't know what time. Not exactly.'

'Mum and Dad were back indoors by half-past seven!' Tim pointed out. '*And* they'd been talking outside. With your mum, Mini. That's hopeful. I don't see Mort would have had enough time . . .'

'He mentioned he drove straight home, after the dentist,' said Ben stubbornly. 'That's good enough for me. And his car wasn't at school, was it, Mini?'

'No, definitely not. Only three cars still in the playground,' Mini agreed. The playground had been turned into a car-park for Parents' Evening. 'None of them was Mort's. Mum looked.'

'But he could have walked from the dentist and still been at school by ten-past seven. Or five-past seven if he drove some of the way, then parked,' said Ludo, with cool logic. 'We've got to pin-point the precise time the person arrived. Was it before or after five-past seven?'

Ben was wrapped in his own thoughts.

'Everybody knows what Mort's car looks like,' he said. 'I'm going to find out where it went. See if I can track its movements last night, after he left the dentist. I'll do it when I take Jax for his walk, after tea.'

'I'll come with you, Ben!' said Tim, eagerly.

'And Mini and I'll talk to our mums,' said Amy. The girls had been whispering together. 'We've got to find out the exact time it – er – *happened*.'

'See what else Mum can remember!' suggested Tim. 'Better leave Dad out of it. Get Mum on her own. Just what exactly did happen? With Marcus's mum, for instance? Mort would never be rude. Not even to her. I don't care what King says!'

Ben nodded agreement. His parents had left the Open Evening before all the excitement, as had Ludo's. So they wouldn't be any help.

'Get the man's description again!' said Ben.

'Any scrap of information. Any clues.

That's what we've got to look for,' stated Ludo. 'And I'm going to check something in the library.'

'Library?' asked Amy, in surprise.

Suddenly there came a faint shout. Mrs Dalladay was calling the twins in for their tea.

'Come on,' said Tim. 'I'm hungry. Meeting over! Again tomorrow, then? A proper long meeting, OK?'

'A brainstorming session!' agreed Ludo. 'We've got to piece the jigsaw together!'

'I'll make some biscuits!' promised Amy. 'To help us think!' Tim picked up the phone book and the radio-phone.

As the others went off, Mini and Ludo lingered behind in the orchard. There had been a shower earlier. Now the sun was shining on the dripping apple trees. Mini found two windfalls in the long, wet grass. They were eaters, rosy-cheeked Cox's. She handed one to Ludo.

'And *did* Mort have gas at the dentist?' she asked him.

'Nope.'

The apples were delicious. As they crunched away, Mini said:

'You were good, Ludo. But what a lie! Saying he might have lost something!'

'Was it?' replied Ludo. 'It was you who gave me the idea in the first place.'

'Lost something! Like what, for instance?'

'How about his memory?' said Ludo.

chapter 6

A Conflict of Evidence

Amy had to wait to get Mum on her own. Dad joined them for tea, from his big study across the hall. He often did. Mr Dalladay worked at home, designing systems as a freelance. His tidy office contained shelves of computer manuals and software, two computers and a fax machine. Mrs Dalladay also worked at home, when time allowed. She was a commercial artist and had a studio upstairs. These two rooms were the only ones in good order – apart from the kitchen.

The Knoll House had been a near ruin when the Dalladays first bought it. The builders came in intermittently to do bits and pieces, but only when there was money to spare. It was still in an awful state. It would be lovely one day. In the mean time the twins were pleased to escape to their caravan sometimes.

The kitchen was fine, however. It was a big family room, very old. The red Aga stove radiated warmth. There were always nice soup smells coming from the pots on top. Mrs Dalladay sometimes made bread in its oven. From the low oak ceiling beams hung bunches of garlic, onions and herbs. The floor was quarry tiled, worn smooth with age. Rugs scattered here and there made the room bright and cheerful. So did the posters on the thick, whitewashed walls. A large oak door led out into the garden. It was from here that Mrs Dalladay had called the twins for tea.

'Nice day at school?' asked Mr Dalladay. He was spreading strawberry jam on his bread, which was home-made today. 'I was quite pleased with your maths books last night, Tim.'

'It was OK, Dad!' said Tim, cramming food into his mouth. The bread was still warm – delicious. 'I scored three times in football!'

Tim could hardly wait to dash off to Ben's house and get started on the car business.

'How was Mr Morton?' asked Mrs Dalladay. 'Oh, *Harry*!' Most of his strawberry jam was landing on his T-shirt.

'He was fine, Mum!' said Amy quickly. She could see Dad's face clouding over. 'He was in a really good mood at assembly this morning!'

'Humph,' said Dad.

'Please can I get down?' Tim asked later, swallowing down his mug of tea. 'Ben's waiting for me. We're going to take Jax for a walk!' Tim crossed his fingers to remind himself of something. He must pick up the club notebook and pencil on his way.

As he shot out of the back door, he gave Amy a meaningful nod. Amy nodded back.

Her chance came a little later, after she'd helped Dad wash up the tea things.

'Got a few things to do in the office,' said Mr Dalladay.

'I'll take Mum up a fresh cup of tea,' said Amy.

Mrs Dalladay had gone upstairs with Harry. She had some artwork to finish off.

Her studio was a light room, with big
windows. It was at the back of the house.
There were good views. You could see the
garden, stretching down to the orchard.
Beyond that you could see the row of
willow trees that lined the stream and just
glimpse the caravan. Her easel was set up
near a window, on her work-table.

Mum was sitting at the easel, dabbing
some colour on a finished drawing. Harry
was on the floor beside her, building a
house with red plastic blocks.

'Lovely, Amy! Thanks!' Mrs Dalladay
took the mug of tea. She sipped it then

placed it on the table, anxious to get on.

'Mum, are you quite sure it was Mr Morton last night?' Amy asked.

'Of course I'm sure!' exclaimed Mrs Dalladay. She was looking at the picture through half-closed eyes, dabbing with the brush. 'In that awful suit he wears. It's so loud!'

'He gave Harry a sweet,' said Amy.

'Did he? How nice. Yes, he did bend down and speak to him. Harry was moping, you see.'

'So Mr Morton was just his normal self when he first appeared?' asked Amy.

'Yes – ' began Mum. Then clammed up.

'I *do* know what happened, Mum!' coaxed Amy. 'Marcus King told Tim, you see. At school today. Marcus said his mum was rude to Mort.'

'Yes. She was. Very. Something about a prize!' Mrs Dalladay pursed her lips and frowned. She didn't approve of Mrs King. 'Something about him not being fit to run the school.'

'What a cheek!' gasped Amy.

'Wasn't it!' agreed Mum, getting into her stride. 'But then Mr Morton yelled at her! Two or three of us rushed over. We thought we'd try and separate them. Then – suddenly – well, he just sort of panicked! Went all crazy, throwing things. And then he just vanished. Fled!'

As Amy stood there, frowning, her mother added: 'Now don't let Daddy hear you talking about this. He's very upset about the whole thing. He's not sure that Mr Morton's really well enough to be, you know . . . well, in charge of you all. He's been wondering if the Governors realize.'

'They do, Mum,' muttered Amy. 'Mrs King *is* a Governor. And he's in trouble.'

'That awful woman's a Governor?' Mrs Dalladay was vague about such things.

'Mum, just another thing. It's really important. When did he first appear? What time was it? *Exactly?*'

'What a funny question.' Mrs Dalladay closed her eyes, trying to remember. 'Well, I know Harry had just started whining. And I was thinking, crikey-it's-time-to-get-him-home. So I looked at the big clock on the wall . . .'

'Yes?' asked Amy eagerly.

'That's right. I can see it now. Just as he walked in the door. It was a quarter-past seven. But you just keep out of this, Amy. I know what you jugs and handles are like!'

'Mum says definitely a quarter-past seven!' Amy whispered down the phone.

'That's about the same as my mum!' replied Mini.

There was a pause as the two friends thought about it. Amy spoke first.

'So he *could* have made it from the dentist. Easy. Even without the car.'

'Yes,' agreed Mini. Another pause. 'D'you know what Ludo thinks, Amy?'

'No?'

'He thinks that after Mort left the dentist, he must have had a black-out.'

Startled, Amy remembered Mort in his office this morning – when he'd asked her and Ben if there'd been any reports of his being seen at school. *He*'d asked *them*. He could tell from Amy's face that there *had* been reports – and he'd been truly shaken. Almost as though . . .

'I've just realized something, Mini!' Amy exclaimed. 'I think that's just what Mr Morton thinks himself!' She hesitated. 'Only there's one little thing that doesn't make sense.'

'What's that?'

'It would be such a funny thing to do – to wear your best clothes to the dentist.'

Tim and Ben bought a bag of chips by Packers Bridge. They shared them with Jax. Ben's collie dog barked eagerly and wolfed them down. The walking was making him hungry.

A mist was settling over the river. Two sea-gulls, up from the coast, were wheeling high above their heads. Hearing their loud cries, Tim tossed a chip on to the parapet of the bridge. They plummeted down on to it.

'Well, nobody saw Mort's car going towards school last night,' said Ben. 'From the dentist, I mean. Didn't think they would have done.'

The dental surgery had been closed since half-past four, of course. But they'd asked at the garage on the corner. Then, tracing the route back to Bridge Street, they'd asked two boys who delivered evening papers and several other people.

'So we make for his house now!' said Tim. 'Mort said he drove straight home. Looks like it's true.'

'We just need to find a witness!' said Ben, confidently.

They both knew the head's house. It was number 28 Clarendon Road, on the far side of town. They'd been there to tea once, after County Junior athletics. They'd like to have gone to Clarendon Road first. But they couldn't go in broad daylight and run the risk of being seen by Mr Morton. So they'd checked the school route first.

Now it was dusk.

It was a long walk.

They strode briskly along by the river then over Abbey Bridge. They took the track which skirted round the abbey precincts, then turned up Abbey Avenue. They walked along the length of the avenue and then turned, at last, into Clarendon Road. Sensing the excitement and tension, Jax barked eagerly.

It was almost dark now, except for the street lamps. It was one of the older roads in the town, lined with trees and handsome Victorian semi-detached houses. They were well spaced and most of them had their own garages. The boys crept along the odd-numbered side of the road. They stopped behind a tree, nearly opposite number 28.

The wooden garage doors were open. Mr Morton's white car was in there. There was no sign of the head. But a slim, fair-haired youth, his son presumably, was washing the car. Toby Morton had his back to them.

There was nobody else around at all. The street looked dead. The boys walked on a little way, in case the youth should see them. Then they stopped and looked back.

'Who on earth are we going to ask?' whispered Ben, in despair. 'We can't very well go knocking on doors.'

'Look!' said Tim. 'That net curtain moved! Somebody's watching the car being washed!'

On this side of the road, in the house bang opposite Mr Morton's, a figure was seated in the front bay window. She was watching what was happening across the road. Her light was on and the boys could see there the silhouette of an elderly lady. She seemed to be knitting. Knitting and watching.

'Wonder if she sits there every night?' said Tim softly, feeling excited. 'Ben, this could be our lucky break!'

'How do we find out?' asked Ben.

They stayed back in the shadows, watching and waiting.

After a while, with much heaving, Toby Morton closed up the garage doors at number 28. The car wash for his father was complete. A bright poster on the front of one garage door started to flap in the wind. It was illuminated by a street lamp. It had a large figure 12 on it. The youth secured the poster more firmly, then went indoors.

'OK,' said Tim, 'I've got an idea. Let's talk to the old lady. We'd better go round the back though. We don't want to be seen from number 28!'

The elderly lady was surprised to see two boys and a dog on her back doorstep.

'If you're the Scouts, they've been already,' she said, apologetically.

'It's a school environment project, ma'am,' said Tim politely. He was glad he'd brought the club notebook and pencil. They looked very business-like. 'Traffic movements in the evening. After six o'clock. D'you get many cars in Clarendon Road? How about last night . . .'

Jax tried to get into the kitchen. He'd seen a meat pie. Ben pulled him back and made him sit down. Ben hardly dared look Tim in the eye! But what skill! And the way he worked the questions round from the general to . . .

That white car opposite, for example.

'Ah, yes. Well, they *often* go out socially in the evening, Mr and Mrs Morton. But she's been away a month. Her mother's ill, you see. Now, let me think . . . yes. Just after seven, that's when the car got back last night. Eh? well, the seven o'clock news had started on the wireless. It was about four minutes past seven. He locked the garage up for the night . . . No. He didn't take the car out again. He always leaves the garage doors open if he's going out again. They're very difficult those doors. They stick.'

Tim heard Ben draw breath.

'Had the driver been to work? Or was it a journey made for social reasons?' asked Tim. 'For instance, was he wearing a smart suit?'

'Smart suit? I should say not! He never wears smart suits. Just his usual old brown clothes. Working late, I dare say. In my young day, if you were in the teaching profession . . .'

'So you think about ten people in the street took their cars out last night?' jerked out Tim. He pretended to note it down. 'But not the people opposite.'

'That's right. Now, would you boys like a biscuit?'

She found them a digestive biscuit each and one for Jax.

But she'd given them much more than that.

Ben and Tim were exultant. They couldn't wait to get home.

chapter 7

Ghost Fever at JVJ

*H*arry was in his little bedroom, in the cot. Amy was reading him a Peter Rabbit story. Then Tim burst in, panting for breath.

'Amy! It wasn't Mort!' he hissed excitedly. 'We've got a witness! It's just like he said. He drove straight home from the dentist yesterday! He put the car in the garage at four minutes past seven and locked it up for the night! He's in the clear!'

Amy stared at Tim, startled.

'Peter Wabbit!' shrieked Harry, furious at the interruption.

'Night, night, Harry!' laughed Tim and raced off again.

He went straight downstairs and

telephoned Ludo. A fierce argument broke out and they both got quite heated. Luckily Mum was busy cooking and Dad had gone to the River Arms.

Ludo had some theory of his own which Tim considered completely crackpot.

'He had a black-out, Tim! Wait till you see this book I got from the library!'

'Ludo, he was at *home*. Mrs Morton's away and his son must have been out. But we've got a witness. The old lady who lives opposite him. Ben and I have thought of a good plan! Why don't we write the head an anonymous letter, telling him about the proof! We can smuggle it into his office tomorrow. We know he must be wondering what to say on Sunday – to the Governors. He *must* be a bit worried. Well, now he won't have to worry any more!'

'Of course he's worried. Poor Mort. Wouldn't you be if you were him?' said Ludo stubbornly. He'd worked very hard on his investigation. Now he was sure his theory was correct. 'Want to bet? It'll be no use smuggling a note into Mr Morton's office tomorrow. I have a feeling he won't be there.'

*

Ludo was right about that, at least. Mr Morton took a day's sick-leave on Friday. It was Mrs Edwards, the deputy head, who took assembly in his place. She gave out the notice about Ben's mug.

'Perhaps the ghost took it!' whispered Paula Harris to her friends in 3B.

Amongst the younger ones, there was ghost fever at JVJ that day. Rumour and counter-rumour swept the corridors.

Meanwhile, in 6A, Anna Patel had got the complete run-down on Mr Morton's recent dental problem.

She'd been sitting behind a bookcase in the library when she'd overheard Mrs Edwards and Mrs Hart whispering about it. It was quite dramatic; not just ordinary toothache.

It appeared that for some time now Mort had been grinding his teeth in his sleep. Actually grinding them together, really hard! It was a sign of stress, they said. It had set up terrible nerve pains in the jaw. There was no cure for it until the dentist could make this special tooth guard for his mouth! You could wear it in your mouth at nights and it stopped you grinding your teeth! So poor Mr Morton had been having really bad nights, and really bad days as well! He'd been doped up with aspirin every day to keep him going. Wasn't it awful.

When Ludo got wind of this, he nodded sagely.

'Well, doesn't that just prove it?' he said to Mini, at lunch-time. 'Deep stress . . . lack of sleep . . . pain-killers. All that could easily lead to a black-out.'

'But now the dentist's cured the problem, why's he off sick?' asked Mini worriedly.

'Having blacked out once, he's worried he'll do it again!' suggested Ludo, looking very unhappy. 'And the dentist *hasn't* cured the problem. He's only cured the symptoms! What's Mort all stressed up about? Why grind his teeth in the first place?'

Ludo had been reading his medical book from cover to cover!

'Ludo,' said Mini, feeling upset, 'you don't think Mort's wondering if he should resign?'

'I don't know,' said Ludo, frowning. 'But you can't have a headmaster who has black-outs, can you? So it's possible. It is possible.'

Ben and Tim would have none of this.

'Your mum's going to look silly at the Governors' meeting,' they told Marcus King. 'When Mr Morton gets there he'll have some proof that he never came to Parents' Evening!'

'Oh, yes?' said Marcus, pityingly. 'Since when can someone prove the impossible?'

And after Marcus had left the classroom, Ludo said: 'Look, you two, I think I agree with him.'

Ben and Tim glowered at Ludo. They collected their books and walked away.

The Handles were in disarray.

Amy just gave a little shiver. She didn't know *what* to think.

The meeting at HQ tonight had been planned as a brainstorming session.

Well, never mind the brains. There was going to be a storm all right.

chapter 8

A Stormy Meeting

'*Do* stop arguing,' sighed Amy. 'Here, have a biscuit.'

She'd baked the biscuits on Thursday night. Then she'd iced them as soon as she'd got home today. Some were iced pink and some white. She thought they looked rather good. She'd arranged them nicely on a large plate, then brought them to the caravan for the meeting.

The others were seated. Ben and Tim on one side of the table, Ludo and Mini on the other. They were taking sides; insulting each other.

Amy set the plate of biscuits down between them.

They didn't even notice. They were

much too busy quarrelling.

'You crackpot, Ludo!' Tim raged.
'According to you then, Mort got home
Wednesday night, locked his car up, had
a black-out, went upstairs . . .'

Ben interrupted.

'. . . no, *ran* upstairs, changed all
his clothes, then *ran* all the way to
school! It's comic, Lu. It's really comic.
He'd have to run like an Olympic
champion.'

'In his best suit and with a lost
memory!' scoffed Tim. 'It's nutty!'

'He might have been able to do it, on a

bike,' said Ludo, stubbornly. 'You've just got closed minds!'

'Stupid!' said Ben.

'Stupid yourself!' retorted Ludo.

'We're supposed to be having a meeting!' exploded Mini suddenly. 'Not quarrelling with each other! *Somebody* appeared at school. There's got to be *some* explanation. You might at least let Ludo read it out – what he's found in the medical book.'

'Yes, let him read it out,' said Amy crossly. She was annoyed that none of them had even noticed her biscuits. 'I want to hear it, even if you two don't.'

'All right, then,' grumbled Tim.

Ludo had the library book in his hand. He opened it, where he'd put the bookmark.

'Thanks,' he said. He pushed his reddish hair out of his eyes. 'I won't read the whole thing. But it's all about severe stress, and – '

'Like people grinding their teeth at night for instance!' Mini pointed out encouragingly.

'– and insomnia, and people losing their memories.'

'What's insomnia?' asked Amy.

'Not being able to sleep,' explained Ludo. 'We all need sleep, like we need food and water and fresh air. If we don't get it, we can crack up. Fainting, amnesia, that sort of thing. Amnesia means loss of memory.'

'Yes, well, what else does it say?' asked Ben impatiently.

'OK! The number one thing is this. Like under hypnosis, people with amnesia sometimes lose their inhibitions . . .'

'Their whats?' asked Tim. 'What are they?'

'Well, the sort of brakes in your head that stop you doing the things you'd secretly love to do,' explained Ludo. 'Things you'd like to do but'd never dare to do as your normal self.'

'Don't you see?' said Mini, excitedly. 'Mrs King's the curse of Mort's life! Yet he's always been careful to be polite to her. Talk about bottled-up feelings! Then on Wednesday night, he had a black-out and really let go! It all fits.'

'Does it?' said Ben, not very impressed.

But Amy was staring at Ludo with great interest.

'Ludo. When you lose your inhibwhat's-its, d'you only do things you secretly *want* to do? I mean, is it possible you'd do something you'd *never* want to do? Even in your secret heart?' she asked.

'Certainly not,' said Ludo. 'The impulse has got to be there in the first place. Buried deep. But Mort *would* secretly want to show Marcus's mum what he thinks of her. Like Mini said – '

'I'm not talking about that!' said Amy, impatiently. 'I'm talking about the Minty Monster!'

'The minty what?' asked Ludo, in surprise.

Tim looked at Amy in delight.

'The person gave Harry a Minty Monster!' he exclaimed. 'It nearly choked him.'

'Mort would never want to do that!' said Amy, with certainty. 'He might have secret feelings against Mrs King. He certainly hasn't got any against our little bruv!'

'Are you *sure* he gave him a gob-stopper?' asked Mini, astonished.

'Quite sure, Mini. I've been meaning to tell you about it. It's the thing I find weirdest of all, when I think about it.'

Ludo was silent.

He looked rather perplexed. He knew that his theory had been struck a serious blow.

Ben reached out a hand and took the nearest biscuit. He scrunched it.

'Delicious biscuits, Amy.' He grinned, and met her eyes with gratitude. 'Well done, Amy. Really brill. Didn't realize I was hungry.'

At his home in Clarendon Road, Mr Morton wasn't in the least bit hungry.

'I've found some curry in the freezer, Dad,' said his son, Toby. 'I'm going to put it in the microwave. Sure you wouldn't like some?'

'Quite sure, Toby,' replied Mr Morton. He was sitting at the polished desk in his study. He'd be glad when his wife got back from Scotland. It had been a very long month. Her mother was on the mend now. He was tired of living out of the deep-freeze! 'Thanks for cleaning the car last night, son,' he added, abstractedly. 'That was a nice surprise.'

'Oh, it was nothing, Dad,' replied Toby, looking embarrassed. He hovered in the doorway. 'I gave the form in today! My tutor was really pleased. Said I'd come to

my senses at last. So you see, he agrees
with you, Dad.'

His father nodded. He was thinking of
the price he was now paying for so much
discord and anxiety. He couldn't bring
himself to discuss it further.

'Had a good day in London?' asked his
son, nervously.

'Satisfactory,' replied Mr Morton. He
had no intention of discussing *that* either.

'Everything all right at school?'

'Now go and have your supper, Toby,'
said Mr Morton, irritably. 'I'm busy.'

The headmaster took a blank sheet of

notepaper from the drawer of his desk. He opened his fountain-pen. He sat staring at the paper for some time, thinking. In London that day, he'd met an old school-friend for lunch. His friend was an important medical man these days.

He'd needed his advice, badly. They'd discussed the whole thing carefully. The whole unnerving thing. They'd both agreed that, in the circumstances, carrying on in this particular job was perhaps not wise. Much as he loved Jug Valley Juniors.

Slowly Mr Morton began to compose a formal letter. He intended to read it out at the Governors' meeting on Sunday. It was a letter of resignation.

chapter 9

Face to Face

'*T*ell you what,' said Ben, looking at the others. 'I know what we can do!'

Ben was always generous in victory.

'What?' asked Ludo, still looking very perplexed.

It had been such a surprise – the business of the sweet. It certainly made the lost memory theory doubtful. If the twins were right about that, then they were all back to square one.

'We'll check out this black-out theory of yours,' said Ben, handsomely. 'We'll check it out once and for all.' He loved action, anyway!

'How?' asked Mini.

'A time trial, of course!' said Ben. He looked pleased with himself. 'We won't run it. We'll do it on our bikes!'

'That's a good idea, Ben!' exclaimed Tim. 'What could be fairer than that?'

Ludo and Mini exchanged gratified looks.

'OK,' nodded Ludo. He wasn't going to let go of his theory completely. Not yet. In spite of his serious doubts, where were they going to find another explanation?

He certainly didn't believe in *ghosts*!

Nor did Mini. It was funny about the gob-stopper of course. But otherwise Ludo's deductions still made sense. Mr Morton *had* been under stress. He'd actually been grinding his teeth! She never knew that people really did that. She thought it was just an expression! Kate Roberts had said he had family problems. Well, maybe Kate was right, after all.

Let's face it – *somebody* had been at school, thought Mini. And the exact double of Mort! How did Ben and Tim explain *that*? And if Mort *didn't* have a black-out, it meant he knew what he'd done and was now trying to cover up.

That's what Marcus King believed. Well, she'd never believe *that*. The search for the truth must continue.

'Agreed, Ben,' said Mini. 'When shall we go?'

Dusk was falling outside. They heard an owl hoot.

'In the morning?' suggested Tim. 'Straight after activities?'

'OK,' said Ben. 'It's only Saturday tomorrow. And the Governors' meeting's not till Sunday. That still gives us plenty of time.'

As far as Ben and Tim were concerned, the time trial was just a formality. It would give them the final piece of proof they needed. And then they'd see to it that Mort found out the good news. That he had the perfect alibi. That he couldn't possibly have been at Jug Valley Juniors on Wednesday evening.

They weren't interested in proving what *had* happened at the Parents' Evening.

That could be left to the Governors.

They were interested in proving what *hadn't* happened – and thus clearing Mr Morton's name.

Unlike Ben and Tim, Amy didn't know which way she wanted the time trial to turn out. To her it was a no-win situation, either way.

But everybody agreed that the biscuits were delicious.

They met at the JVJ bike sheds at 12 noon on Saturday, after activities. There were clubs at school on Saturday mornings. Ludo belonged to Chess Club and the other four to Gym Club. They'd all brought their bikes to school.

Ludo, Mini and Amy gazed at the green sports field. It was a warm, still day. They were all thinking how much they loved JVJ and having Mr Morton as headmaster. The idea of his resigning, no longer being here, was unthinkable!

Tim and Ben weren't interested in such morbid thoughts.

'Are we ready, then?' asked Tim, as they wheeled their bikes through the playground. They made for the school gates that opened on to Bridge Street, not the Back Lane ones. This was going to be good fun, thought Tim.

Mr Morton had left the dentist at seven sharp. He was back home in Clarendon Road four minutes later. That figured. He'd put the car away and locked up the garage. Another minute. He'd been wearing ordinary clothes. He needed to find a shirt, knot his tie, change into his suit. Four minutes? If he moved fast. That'd make it nine minutes past seven.

The car had remained locked in the garage. He could either have sprinted to school, or used a bike. (Did he even have a bike? The more you thought about it, the dafter it seemed! thought Tim.) But OK, of the two, the bike would be quicker. He was seen in the school hall at seven-fifteen. He'd have needed at least a minute to dump the bike, then make his way to the hall. He'd have needed to reach these gates by seven-fourteen!

Fourteen take away nine = five.

'And we're all agreed on five minutes?' said Tim. They'd discussed it earlier. 'If it takes more than five minutes, it can't be done.'

'We're doing the journey in reverse,' Ludo pointed out. 'Bridge Street's uphill, going this way.'

It was a fair comment and typical of Ludo's lateral thinking.

'But Abbey Avenue's *downhill*, going this way,' Ben realized. 'So that evens it out.'

'And the rest's on the flat, isn't it?' said Mini. 'All along by the river?'

'Good,' said Amy. She was anxious to get going, get it over with. 'So from school to Mort's house'll take just about the same time as from his house to school. That's agreed.'

'Time check,' said Ludo, looking at his watch.

They all checked. It was 12.05.

'Go!' shouted Ben.

Some of the Gym Club members watched the 'off'. What was happening? It looked as though these five were having a bike race!

Ben powered ahead up Bridge Street, moving through the gears of his old battered bike. Tim was close behind.

Amy was next, then Ludo. Mini was bringing up the rear, her short little legs pumping up and down. It was a stiff climb. She gasped a bit at the pace that Ben and Tim were setting. She had to admire them. There was no cheating here!

Amy was proud of them, too.

At Packers Bridge they turned left along The Waterfront. It was a flat, easy ride all along the river bank as far as Abbey Bridge. Now the boys really powered along, opening up a big gap. Amy couldn't keep up on her old red bike. Ludo and Mini were a long way behind.

By the time Ben and Tim went over Abbey Bridge, they'd lost the others completely.

They caught the traffic-lights at green on the far side of the bridge. They sped through them, skirting the bottom of

Cheap Street. Then they turned left down the cycle-track that led round the abbey precincts. They were puffing hard by the time they shot into Abbey Avenue and were pleased to be able to coast downhill. Then, left into Clarendon Road, another hard burst of pedalling, and –

They were there!

'Phew!' said Ben, braking hard, well past number 28.

A moment later, Tim's brakes screeched alongside.

'Nine minutes!' gasped Tim, looking at his watch. It was 12.14.

'Can't be done!' they both cried in triumph.

They dragged their cycles up a driveway out of sight. Then they crouched there, heads between knees, until they got their breath back. Nine minutes! And it had been worth every second.

'Shake, partner!' grinned Tim. He took Ben's sweaty hand and pumped it up and down. 'So we've proved it. It can't be done.'

'Ludo had better take his book back to the library!' laughed Ben.

Amy arrived next, gulping for breath.

'Can't be done, Amy!' exclaimed Tim. 'Not in five minutes. It's taken us nine!'

'Mort would have had to sprout wings!' chortled Ben.

'Sssh,' said Amy anxiously, gazing round. 'Which is his house? He mustn't see us.'

'It's all right. It's that one back there. Look, the garage doors are open. The car's gone. He's out somewhere.'

Amy looked relieved.

Ludo and Mini turned into Clarendon Road and came pedalling along. They were taking their time. They knew they'd lost the argument.

'You've proved your point!' said Ludo. He didn't need to check his watch again. The five minutes had been up even before the Abbey Bridge traffic-lights!

Tim was scrabbling in his saddle-bag, looking for something. Mini was baffled.

'Which is the old lady's house?' she asked. 'Are you sure about her? Are you sure she knows that Mort didn't take his car out again? How can you be sure?'

Tim laughed. He indicated the house across the road from Mr Morton's. The net curtain had just twitched. They could all see the outline of the figure seated in the bay window, downstairs at the front.

'Because she's an old lady and she's

bored and she sits in that window all the time. Bet you she never misses a thing,' he said. 'Why don't you go and ask her yourself, Mini?'

Mini shook her head, wryly. 'I was only asking. What's that you've got, Tim?'

'Tim's composed a note,' said Ben. They'd discussed it together, before Gym Club. 'We got it all ready – in case! Tim's made it anonymous. So's not to embarrass him.'

They all crowded round and read Tim's message. It was written in block capitals:

DEAR SIR

IN CASE YOU ARE WORRIED ABOUT WHAT HAPPENED ON WEDNESDAY NIGHT, PLEASE ASK THE OLD LADY OPPOSITE. SHE SAW YOU PUT YOUR CAR AWAY AT FOUR MINUTES PAST SEVEN AND NOT GO OUT AGAIN.

YOURS SINCERELY

HANDS
(I.E. FIVE WELL-WISHERS)

'Shall we take a vote?' asked Tim.

They all raised their arms in favour.

'The headmaster could *not* have come to school,' said Amy. 'Not in person.' It didn't really need saying. It was now obvious beyond doubt.

Even though she, Ludo and Mini were still very, very puzzled.

Tim put the note in its envelope. He sealed the envelope and wrote on it:

To: MR DEREK MORTON.
<u>PRIVATE</u>

'OK,' said Ben nervously. 'Let's put it through his letter-box. While he's still out.'

'Quick, then!' said Amy.

Leaving their bikes in the driveway, they crept two houses along to number 28. Ludo and Mini hung back, by the open garage doors. Ludo's attention had been caught by something. A flapping poster, with his sister's name on it. He'd glimpsed the same poster up on Anya's bedroom wall.

The other three opened the side gate into the garden and went through. Tim and Ben led the way. The path from the side gate to Mr Morton's front door went right past his sitting-room window. As she followed the boys, Amy noticed that the sash window was slightly open at the bottom. Odd, that. It proved that Mr Morton wouldn't be gone for long!

She stared at something on the window-sill inside.

Then a shiver ran down her spine.

'Tim! Ben!' she gasped. 'Come back here a minute!'

The boys rushed back to see what was wrong. Tim was still holding the envelope. Amy had gone a sickly white colour.

There was a bag of sweets on the window-sill. Big ones, black-and-white striped.

'Minty Monsters!' gulped Tim.

Amy just continued to stare at them. Mort couldn't have come to school *in person*. But the Minty Monsters! How did you explain *those*?

'Then it *was* a ghost,' she whispered, feeling faint.

As Amy swayed slightly, Ben gripped her under the elbow. He was determined to be sensible.

'Stop it, Amy. Ghosts don't carry real live sweets around with them! Watch this!'

He pressed his face against the window. Looking down, he eased his hand through the gap at the bottom. He fumbled for the sweet bag. 'They look real to me! You can taste one, if you like – '

Suddenly a large pale hand appeared. It closed over the bag. Then a pale face pressed itself against the inside of the pane. Ben stared into the face and the face stared back. It was gaunt and high-cheek-boned, with light bushy eyebrows.

Now it was Ben's turn to feel a shiver down the spine.

He knew that face! It wasn't a real face! It was a long-ago face from a faded photograph.

Ben recoiled.

Amy screamed.

The face shouted: 'Leave my sweets alone!'

And they backed away, fast.

chapter 10

One Mystery Solved . . .

*T*im backed straight into Ludo and Mini, at the open side gate.

'That sounded like Mort's voice!' gasped Ludo, as Tim cannoned into him.

'It wasn't him,' said Tim, heart thudding.

'What happened?' exclaimed Mini.

She put an arm round Amy. She could see her best friend was trembling.

'There's some Minty Monsters in there, Mini! What are they *doing* there?'

Ben, too, was more shaken than Ludo had ever seen him.

'There's someone in there! He's just like the photograph, Lu,' he gulped. 'It's as if the photo's come to life.'

'What photo?' rapped out Ludo.

'The one in the head's office, at school. Of him long ago. When he was young.'

Mini and Ludo exchanged startled glances. Something clicked. Of course! Thanks to what Ben had just said, they'd both had exactly the same brilliant thought at once. It was like telepathy.

'Now who's the one with the crackpot theory?' said Ludo to Ben. 'There might be a simpler one. Here, come and have a look at this poster.'

They went into a huddle round the poster on the garage door.

Somewhere behind them, the front door creaked open.

'You kids still hanging around? I want to know what you're up to.'

The Handles & Spouts whirled round. As the figure advanced towards them, tiny little Mini pulled herself up to her full height. She was tense, but determined.

'We'll tell you,' said Mini, with great dignity. 'And then we want to ask *you* a few questions!'

It was Sunday afternoon. The Governors were waiting for the headmaster. They were sitting round in a circle in the panelled drawing-room of Raleigh House. Sir David Grateley's Elizabethan home in the abbey close was rather grand.

The room was hushed. They'd just seen the white car arrive. He'd be here at any moment.

Then the door to the drawing-room opened.

'In here, sir,' said the maid.

The plump, bearded figure walked into their midst, wearing the brown-and-white checked suit for the occasion. Instead of taking the empty chair, Mr Morton strode across to Marcus King's mother. He bowed.

'I'd like to apologize for my horrible behaviour on Wednesday night,' he said.

'Thank you, Mr Morton,' said Mrs King. She was wearing her best purple suit and a large hat. 'But obviously we are all deeply disturbed.'

The Chairman of the Governors eyed him angrily.

'I'm glad to see that your memory's decided to return, Derek.'

'It never went,' said a deep, friendly voice from the doorway.

The Governors gasped in shock and looked round.

A second plump, bearded figure was

95

walking towards them! If this one hadn't
been wearing different clothes, plain brown
trousers and a corduroy jacket, they'd have
sworn they were seeing double!

It was the second figure who was the
real headmaster.

He walked over to the first figure. He
clapped a hand on its check-suited padded
shoulder.

'I'm afraid this is a different Mr
Morton,' said the head. His 'double' was
already pulling off a false beard. He then
removed a brown wig – and plugs of
cotton wool from inside his cheeks. His face

no longer looked plump.

They were looking at a gaunt-faced, fair-haired youth. His only likeness to the headmaster (and it was a remarkable one) lay in the distinctive high cheek-bones, the straight nose and the bushy brown eyebrows. The eyebrows in fact were darkened down with make-up, as they had been on Wednesday.

'My son, Mr Toby Morton,' said the headmaster, 'I'm ashamed to say.'

'Good grief,' gasped Sir David Grateley, glancing from father to son. 'What was it? A practical joke? A joke that went wrong?'

'Rather more than that, Sir David,' said Mort. 'It had a serious purpose at the time. But it certainly went wrong.'

Toby had taken off the suit jacket now, together with the fat padded waistcoat he'd been wearing underneath. He bundled the wig and beard inside them. The Governors were watching, open-mouthed. Especially Mrs King.

'By jove, you're quite skinny, as well!' said Sir David. He was feeling very, very relieved. There was a light in his eye.

'All right, Toby. Take all those things outside and wait in the car,' said the headmaster. 'They can go back to college again tomorrow. Off you go. I have some explaining to do.'

But about one thing his son was determined. He turned back to Mrs King.

'I've apologized to you. Now I think you should apologize to my father,' he said quietly. 'Just because your son didn't win that prize, you said my father wasn't fit to run his school.'

Toby marched out. As he went, all eyes turned to Marcus King's mother. She was blushing deeply. It was obvious that the young fellow was telling the truth.

His father, in spite of all that had passed, suddenly felt very proud of him.

Mr Morton had indeed been under strain. His wife's mother, whom they all loved, had been seriously ill. While his wife went to Scotland to nurse her, Mr Morton had been left to run the household for a month. A month in which their son Toby had suddenly become a horrible young rebel.

Toby was a clever boy, their only child. He was his father's pride and joy; he longed for him to go to university. Now suddenly Toby was refusing to fill in the form! Joining the Jugmouth College Drama Society had gone to his head. He wanted to drop out of school and become an actor!

If only Mrs Morton had been at home, together they might have talked him round. Instead, father and son quarrelled endlessly. Toby couldn't act! He'd been rejected for a part in *Twelfth Night*. As Ludo and Mini had seen at the bottom of the college poster (in tiny type), he'd had to settle for the job of assistant wardrobe master! He was ruining his life, thinking he could be an actor.

It was enough to make a father grind his teeth! And that led to tooth trouble, sleepless nights and aspirin-filled days. The more bad-tempered Mr Morton became, the more stubborn was Toby.

Then, the morning after the dentist (and at last a good night's sleep!), something wonderful happened. With the deadline looming for his university entrance form, Toby caved in. An amazing change of heart! Pale-faced and subdued at breakfast, he'd informed his father that he'd been right all along. He didn't want to be an actor, after all! It was breath-taking.

Of course, Toby daren't confess: that he'd borrowed a Shakespearian disguise and his father's suit and been in to JVJ.

It had seemed such a brilliant idea at the time, to impersonate his father.

He'd make a brief appearance at Parents' Evening, while Dad was at the dentist. A few smiles and handshakes all round. He'd pass it off easily! How amazed his father would be, when he told him! How impressed! He'd have to admit that he was wrong. That he, Toby Morton, was a truly great actor.

Only it had all gone horribly wrong.

When that dreadful woman had been rude about Dad, he'd lost his temper! His first real test of acting ability – and he'd failed it. Then, seeing people bearing down on him, he'd panicked! It was easy enough to dress up like Dad. But he'd no idea how to act like him. He'd hurled stuff around – anything to create a diversion. And fled.

It was a moment of truth. He'd slunk behind the school sheds, where his rucksack and bike were hidden. He'd removed his disguise, put it back in the rucksack and waited till the coast was clear. Then he'd cycled home. His taste for acting was cured.

He longed to confess to Dad. But he was too scared. He went about in fear and trembling, hoping it would all blow over.

He hoped it hadn't caused trouble for Dad.

If only he'd known! Trouble wasn't the word for it. Not for one moment had the headmaster guessed the truth. He would never have dreamt that his son could do something so outrageous!

All Mort knew was that he'd felt very groggy after the dentist. It was easy to convince himself that he must have had a black-out. And he was going to resign.

But Toby knew nothing. He didn't even know that a Governors' meeting had been called.

Until Handles & Spouts told him.

He'd never had such a telling-off in his life. About the Minty Monster, too.

'It could have choked our baby brother!' Amy scolded. 'It really could have choked him!'

... and then Another

*T*he news swept through Jug Valley Juniors on Monday morning. It was a great relief, especially to the younger ones. There hadn't been a ghost, after all. It had all been a practical joke! Wasn't that amazing?

Of course, Handles & Spouts weren't quite convinced by Toby Morton's explanation. That it had just been a joke. Ludo had asked his sister about the head's son. Well, Anya said, there were loads of people in the college drama society. Toby Morton was quite a minor member. But, yes, he *was* the rather intense type. Had he nursed secret dreams of being an actor? Well, maybe. Who could tell.

Mini checked up on that quarrel Kate Roberts's mother had overheard in the chemist. And, yes, it had been between father and son.

So, putting two and two together, Hands half-guessed the truth. But, as Ben said, it was none of their business anyway.

Mort was himself again. JVJ was back to normal. That was all that mattered.

Marcus King even had the sense to apologize. He seemed in quite a good mood. His mother was threatening to resign as a Parent Governor. She was saying she wasn't appreciated! Well, here's hoping.

And the chocolate biscuits that morning were delicious. Mort invited the five of them to his study, at break. He was even wearing his best suit for the occasion.

'Just a word of thanks,' he said. 'I see I've got a few bright sparks in Class 6A!'

Mrs Hart wheeled in the trolley. On it was a plate piled high with chocolate biscuits and six mugs of hot tea.

Five of the mugs were a light brown colour. The sixth was a darker brown.

'Where did that mug come from?' asked Ben.

'From the cupboard with the others,'

replied the school secretary. 'We don't normally use this many.'

'It's my *pottery*!' said Ben.

They all stared at it.

'Extraordinary!' whispered Mort. 'Are you saying it's your missing piece of work, Ben? But it looks just like a proper mug . . . Oh, dear. I *think* I can guess what must have happened.'

It was those aching teeth again. Last Tuesday afternoon, he'd been working late. He'd been in such a blur. He needed to take some more aspirin. Yes, he must have wandered through and picked it up from the trolley without giving it a second glance – thinking only that he needed some water to take with the aspirin! He must have washed the mug up afterwards at the sink. Then automatically dried it and put it away with the others! All the time his mind far away, on other things . . .

'Well, well, well, Ben!' said Mort, looking rather red-faced. 'To think I never noticed anything special about it. I just mistook it for one of *our* mugs!' He put his hands round the mug and took a sip of tea. 'But what a compliment, my boy. What a professional job!'

At that they all laughed – and felt very proud of Ben's mug.

Ben took it home to show his parents, complete with gold star. After that, it would go to Club HQ.

And the twins took home chocolate biscuits for Harry. Mort said he deserved some. The little boy fell on the bag in delight.

'Shocklet biscuits!' he said. Then, about to put one to his mouth, he looked anxiously at his father.

'It's all right, Harry. You can eat them this time,' smiled Dad.

'I've just realized something,' said Amy.

105

'He must have a funny picture of school!'

'Yes,' said Tim. 'He must think it rains chocolate biscuits at JVJ.'

'Well, a little boy can have his dreams!' laughed Mum. 'Can't he?'

Also by Anne Digby

'Far better than the run-of-the-mill sub-teen adventure story, the Jill Robinson series combines racy plot with well observed characters and supple writing' – *The Good Book Guide to Children's Books*

ME, JILL ROBINSON AND THE TELEVISION QUIZ

Moving to Haven is full of unexpected excitements for the Robinson family. But for Jill, making friends with the high-spirited daughter of the town's mayor makes it all worthwhile. However, Melinda isn't everyone's favourite person, least of all her father's. So when she gets the chance to compete in a television quiz, she really hopes that at last he will be proud of her. But it isn't that simple.

ME, JILL ROBINSON AND THE SEASIDE MYSTERY

Keeping an eye on her younger brother Tony certainly makes the Robinsons' seaside holiday an exciting one for Jill. Why does he keep disappearing on his own, and who is his new friend, Sam? Dad gets more and more angry with Tony, so Jill and her best friend Lindy try to solve the mystery, only to find themselves in real trouble.

ME, JILL ROBINSON AND THE CHRISTMAS PANTOMIME

Jill's sister, Sarah, is helping Roy Brewster produce the Youth Club's Christmas panto and Jill is dying for a leading role. It looks set to be great fun for Jill and Lindy, until the Runcorn boys get involved and spoil it for everyone. But Jill discovers that their leader, Big Harry, isn't as tough as he makes out.

ME, JILL ROBINSON AND THE SCHOOL CAMP ADVENTURE

Looking after Cu, a stray dog, certainly makes school camp on a remote Scottish island exciting for Jill and Lindy. The scheming Rita is determined to get them into trouble and Miss Rawlings threatens to take Cu away from them. But when Rita goes missing on the mysterious island it is only Cu who can find her.

ME, JILL ROBINSON AND THE PERDOU PAINTING

Jill is really excited when Polly Pudham invites her home for tea, because 'Pud' lives in the most expensive road in Haven. But why is Jill so interested in the oil painting Polly's father has just bought? And what happens when Jill's sister Sarah goes to the Pudhams' cocktail party to see the painting – what is she *supposed* to have done? There are times when the trouble caused by this obscure Frenchman's painting makes Jill and her sister wish they had never laid eyes on it in the first place.

ME, JILL ROBINSON AND THE STEPPING STONES MYSTERY

Feelings in Haven Youth Club run high when it is decided how to spend its hard-earned money. Not everyone is in favour of Roy Brewster's cracking idea to transform the river at the stepping stones bend . . . Then the bridge-building project is sabotaged! But who could have done it? Sir Harry, the local landowner, Jill's brother, Tony, or perhaps someone from the club? Jill and Lindy are determined to find out.

By Alan Davidson

A FRIEND LIKE ANNABEL

Thirteen-year-old Annabel Fidelity Bunce is the wonder of Addendon – adored by her best friend Kate, considered by many of her fellow pupils in 3G at Lord Willoughby's School to be off her head and warily tolerated by teachers and other adults of the town. These five riotously funny, wickedly observant stories prove that with a friend like Annabel life is certainly never dull.

JUST LIKE ANNABEL

Taking sides with a bored donkey against Mrs da Susa and Mrs Stringer, pillars of Addendon, Annabel and Kate are soon on the trail of the Franks–Walters enigma. With her innocent but exasperating persistence, Annabel discovers that all is not as it appears at Addendon Court. In the second story Annabel inexplicably adapts a 'new attitude' to life.

EVEN MORE LIKE ANNABEL

'There'll be a reign of terror,' Annabel predicts when the repellent Julia Channing is appointed Monitor of the Band Room (the school's Junior Leisure and Recreation Centre). And apparently there is! In the second story, Annabel plays a central role in Addendon Town Council's spectacular television debut.

THE NEW, THINKING ANNABEL

In these three stories Annabel, in her inimitable manner, struggles to apply some thought to her actions, with absurdly funny results.

LITTLE YEARNINGS OF ANNABEL

What's the reason, Kate wonders, for Annabel's desperate desire to get into the Guinness Book of Records? Is it really because of what Auntie Lucy Loxby said about Mozart? Or what the careers master said about her future? Or what her last term's report said about her progress? Or something else . . .? Two more funny and poignant stories.